RETURN *of the* OSPREY

Patricia Mason

Illustrated by

Christopher Bateman

Cover illustration by
Christopher and **Robert Bateman**

H A R B O U R   P U B L I S H I N G

FOREWORD
Robert Bateman

For as long as I can remember, I have been an artist and naturalist. All little kids enjoy art and nature but, sadly, many give up that interest. I never gave it up and in fact my interest and activities grew stronger through the years. Now, as a grandfather, I still feel the magic of that childhood pleasure in nature every day. The complicated web of the natural world is like a miracle, and we live in the middle of it. We only have to look and listen and we will never be bored.

In *Return of the Osprey*, Joseph's father teaches him how to appreciate the wonders of nature and this appreciation gives Joseph delight and comfort for the rest of his life. But the story also shows that nature can give the kind of joy it gives Joseph only if it stays healthy. Too often natural places like Joseph's marshlands are damaged by careless people. Wild creatures like Osprey and Raccoons disappear, and people can no longer experience joy in their presence.

That need not be the end of the story. People can create another kind of miracle by helping places like Maplewood Flats to become healthy homes for wildlife once again. *Return of the Osprey* is a hopeful story, made even better by the fact that Maplewood Flats is a real place and that the miraculous rebirth described here really did occur.

I think we should all learn about the natural kind of miracles, and that is why my son Christopher and I decided to work together to help bring this book to you. We hope you find it as much fun as we did.

One sunny day in the springtime many years ago, in the place we now call North Vancouver, an old man took his grandson Joseph down to the inlet to fish. Joseph was only five years old and more interested in playing than fishing, so when the old man had filled his bag with fish, he gathered some stones along the beach and showed Joseph a trick.

"Grandfather!" Joseph shouted. "It's like magic the way the stones jump on the water!"

He gathered some stones of his own to make them jump. But no matter how many times he tried, he could only make the stones bounce once, not two or three times as his grandfather had done.

After a while he lost interest and went to sit with his grandfather, who was now resting against a rock and peacefully smoking his pipe.

"Look, Grandfather!" he cried. "It's like magic the way the smoke from your pipe makes rings in the air."

"Magic is all around us," Grandfather answered. "Come with me and I will show you some of nature's magic."

"No! No!" said Joseph. "Nature is just trees and things. Show me some more magic tricks."

"If you come with me, I will show you a trick," said Grandfather, and he took Joseph's hand and led him away from the beach over the marshes toward the forest. Stopping beside the bushes and shrubs at the edge of the forest, Grandfather said, "Do you remember the last time we came here and I showed you my secret trail?"

"Yes, yes. Let's walk along it again—that was fun," said Joseph.

"Ah, but where is it?" asked Grandfather. "See if you can find it."

Joseph looked and looked but the

entrance to the trail, which had started at a point between two very large maple trees, had disappeared. Then he looked more carefully. Everything looked different from the last time they had been here. It was as if an unseen hand had changed things around, like moving furniture in a room. He looked some more, then turned around. But Grandfather had disappeared, and the bright sun suddenly went behind a cloud. Joseph shivered. He felt cold and a little afraid.

"Grandfather, Grandfather. Where are you?" Joseph heard no answering call, only birdsong and a rather strange whistling sound. Crying quietly but trying to be brave, he ran up and down the edge of the forest, trying to find the entrance to the trail. Finally, in desperation, he pushed his way through the dense bush, crying, "Grandfather, Grandfather, where are you?" Brambles scratched his face and arms but Joseph struggled on. Then, after pushing one more scratchy branch out of the way, he suddenly found himself in a sunny opening and there, standing in front of him with a big smile on his face, was Grandfather.

"You wanted to see a trick, didn't you?" he asked, hugging Joseph. "Well, this is one of nature's greatest magic tricks. One she performs every year. Do you remember, the last time we were here it was wintertime? The branches

were bare, so it was easy to see our secret path. Now it's springtime and the leaves on the branches have covered up our trail. Nature has done her conjuring trick again."

"It's like everything has been moved," said Joseph.

"No. Just changed," said Grandfather, leading Joseph along the trail. "It shows that everything is not as it seems. Nature is never dull. She is always changing, and always has something wonderful to show us."

The forest was filled with the sound of birds, and Joseph liked the way the tall, shady trees made him feel fresh and cool after the hot sun of the beach. Grandfather showed him five different kinds of trees, which he could recognize by looking at their leaves. Joseph felt the shape of each leaf and repeated the names after his grandfather: "Maple, Cottonwood, Alder, Sitka Spruce, Western Red Cedar."

Then Grandfather pointed to a branch. "Look how carefully the spider has made her web. See the pattern made out of hundreds of shiny strands?"

"But I can knock it down easily," said Joseph, raising his hand.

"Stop! Would you wish someone to knock our house down? Think of all the work the spider has done to build her home. That web is a small miracle. It may look fragile and weak, but each strand is very strong in the spider's world."

"What is a miracle?" Joseph wanted to know.

"A miracle is like magic—something that doesn't seem possible. Something so marvellous, so surprising that people can hardly believe it."

"Can people make miracles?" said Joseph.

"Of course. Didn't I just make stones bounce on the water and smoke circles in the air?" asked Grandfather. "People hold within them the same magic that is within nature. We are all part of the same great spirit. One day you will know what I mean."

But Joseph had stopped suddenly. He could hear that strange whistling sound again.

"Ah, that is another of nature's miracles," said Grandfather. "Come, I will show you." But instead of continuing down the trail, Grandfather turned around and started walking back toward the beach.

Joseph followed, wondering what on earth the strange noise could be, and whether he felt frightened.

Grandfather stood on the beach, looking up into the sky. "Look," he said. "There, coming toward us, can you see?"

Joseph looked into the sky, but the sun was too bright. He shaded his eyes with his hand and suddenly saw what Grandfather was talking about. Off in the distance, slowly getting closer and closer, were two large, dark

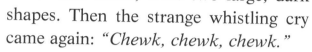

shapes. Then the strange whistling cry came again: *"Chewk, chewk, chewk."*

"But they're not miracles," Joseph said. "They're just birds!"

"Those birds perform a miracle every year," Grandfather said. "They were born here and they return every year to the same nesting place, to find food and have families. They will do that every year until they die because every year they hear a voice inside them—a special voice calling them home."

"Why do they go away?" Joseph asked.

"To find the sun, because that is where the food is. They left here at the end of last summer when it started to get cold and followed the sun for thousands of miles."

"Where do they find it?" Joseph asked.

"In countries far away that are warm while we are having our winter. Hundreds of birds like those stay in the warm countries, then return home every spring to build nests and have families. It is called migration, and it is one of nature's miracles."

Then Grandfather told Joseph how in springtime all the different kinds of birds always came back to the mudflats and marshes where there was plenty of food for them and plenty of places to build their nests.

"Chewk-chewk-chewk," came the whistling cry again.

Then one of the birds was right above Joseph and he saw how big it was. From the tip of one wing, across the bird's back to the tip of the other wing, was about the length of a man. As he watched, the bird made a circle in the sky, then swooped down and fluttered above the water, crying, *"Seek-pseek, seek-pseek."*

"What is the bird called?" asked Joseph.

"They call it the Osprey," said Grandfather, "although I have also heard it called Fish Hawk because it eats mostly fish and looks like a hawk. She is fishing now. See how her beady yellow eyes are searching for fish while she hovers above the sea."

Suddenly the Osprey tucked her wings into a *V* shape above her back and dived. There was a splash, then she disappeared.

Joseph waited.

"Look, there she is," he yelled with excitement as the Osprey rose out of the water, her white breast glinting in the sunlight. The underneath part of the bird was mostly white, mixed with a bit of brown and grey. But the feathers on her back were dark brown, and her white head and face were streaked with black marks. In the Osprey's sharp curved talons was a fish.

"She's taking our fish," Joseph cried.

"No, there is plenty for everyone," said Grandfather. "The fish are returning in huge numbers this year."

"Do the fish migrate too?" Joseph asked.

"Some of them, yes. They hear a voice inside them telling them to return to the place where they were born, just as the Osprey and the other birds that migrate hear the voice. But when the fish come back, it is to lay their eggs and die. It is the cycle of life and death."

"Look, there is another Osprey," shouted Joseph.

"That is the male—the female Osprey's mate. They are happy to be home," said Grandfather.

"Where will they live?"

"Those birds will find a tree with branches over the water," Grandfather replied, "and build a huge nest out of seaweed, bones and twigs. We will come here again and watch them building it. Soon the mother bird will lay eggs and then chicks will hatch out, and they also will have the special voice inside them."

"So will they always come back here—to this place?"

The old man thought carefully for a moment. "As long as they can find a place to build their nest, and lots of food," he said.

Then Grandfather saw something that made him smile. "Our dancing friends have also returned," he said. "Look, see how they weave patterns in the air."

Joseph saw two birds soaring and dipping in the sky, their purple-blue feathers shining in the sunlight.

"That's the bird they call the Purple Martin," Grandfather said.

One of the birds started building a nest in the hole of a dead tree while the other one continued to make patterns in the air.

"He looks as if he is just enjoying himself, but he's actually busy catching flying insects to eat," Grandfather explained. "Ah...all this talk of food is making me hungry."

Joseph was glad when Grandfather gave him a piece of dried fish, some salmonberries and bread to eat. He ate until he felt very full and the warmth of the sun made him sleepy. Then he lay down and closed his eyes.

When Joseph opened his eyes, Grandfather had gone. He was all alone by the water's edge and everything looked different. Was Grandfather hiding again?

Then he heard the *"Chewk-chewk"* cry of the Osprey—but this time he also heard something else.

"Chewk-chewk. We cannot stay this year. The tree we build our nest in every spring has gone. There are too many people on the beach and we cannot get near the sea to fish. We'll have to find somewhere else."

"Tchew-wew, pew, pew—wait for us. We'll fly with you," called the Purple Martins. "The old rotten tree at the edge of the marsh has been cut down and there is nowhere for us to build our nest."

Two Osprey flew over Joseph's head, their huge wings making dark shadows on the water. Behind them, darting here and there, were the purple-blue birds Grandfather had called Purple Martins. Joseph suddenly felt very alone and cold and frightened.

"Don't be afraid, my child," he heard Grandfather's voice say in the distance. "You have been dreaming..."

Joseph rubbed his eyes and sat up slowly. "But I heard the birds. They said they had nowhere to build their homes. What does it mean?" he asked.

Grandfather thought for a minute, then said, "I think you have had a vision—you have seen something from the future."

After that day, Joseph and his grandfather spent many days at the inlet, exploring the maple woods, the marshes and the huge stretches of beach called mudflats. Each time they went there was something new to learn. Grandfather told Joseph that the freshwater marshes, the mudflats and the sea each provided different kinds of food for different kinds of birds, and he began to teach Joseph how to recognize these birds. The long-legged ones whose beaks were perfect for picking tiny animals called amphipods and mudworms out of the mudflats; the curly-toed ones whose feet were perfect for hanging onto the reeds in the marshes, and the diving, swooping, crying birds who found their food in the air and the sea. The seashore was Joseph's favourite place because that is where, each spring, he would see the Osprey and the Purple Martins. He liked to look along the shore of the Burrard Inlet where the mudflats and marshes stretched for miles.

But just as Joseph's grandfather had told him, nothing remains the same forever. Each year, as spring followed winter, Joseph grew up a little more as he changed from a child into a man. He married and soon had children of his own. Life changed in many different ways and there never seemed to be enough time for visits to the beach.

But Joseph always remembered what he had learned from his grandfather, especially about migration and the other miracles of nature. And he never forgot his vision of the Osprey and the Purple Martins losing their homes.

As the years passed, Joseph realized sadly that his vision was coming true. The birds and animals really were losing their homes as humans began to change the land along the inlet. Machines dug out the mudflats for boats to come in and dredge for gravel, the marshes were filled in and many of the maple trees were cut down to make way for gravel mining.

One spring Joseph took his son down to the beach. He wanted to show him the Osprey and Purple Martins building their nests and catching their food. But instead of birds, all they saw were huge carpets of logs, called booms, tied to poles in the sea. Joseph listened for the *"Chewk-chewk"* of the Osprey and the *"Pchew, pchew, wew, pew pew"* of the Purple Martins, but all he could hear was the sound of machines.

Every spring Joseph went down to the inlet to see if the Ospreys and Purple Martins had returned, but they never did. And one day he decided he would not go again.

Sadly, he also stopped believing in magic and miracles. Joseph packed his bags and moved away with his wife and children, to a place far away from the Inlet.

Many years later, when he was a very old man, Joseph dreamed he was back at the inlet with his grandfather once again. In the dream he heard Grandfather say, "Where will you go now that all the marshes and mudflats along the Inlet have gone?" But there was no one there. Who was Grandfather talking to?

Then Joseph heard a familiar sound: *"Chewk, chewk."* It was the Osprey, flapping their huge wings over Grandfather and making their strange cry.

"We have heard of a special place—a place where humans are making a miracle. Come, we will show you."

In the dream Joseph saw his grandfather lift slowly off the ground and, as Joseph watched in amazement, the old man started to fly down the inlet surrounded by several pairs of Osprey and Purple Martin. He heard his grandfather's laugh mixed with the cries of the birds:

"Chewk-chewk-chewk," "Tchew-wew—pew-pew." Joseph watched them get smaller and smaller, then realized that the birds and the man had become one with the huge yellow sun.

He suddenly remembered something grandfather had once told him: "The beasts and birds, the trees, the people. We are all part of the same great spirit... One day you will know what I mean." In his dream Joseph started to remember what Grandfather had said about miracles...

Then he woke up.

"What a fool I am, to dream about a special place for the birds and animals made by humans!" he thought. "The marshes and mudflats along the inlet have been destroyed by humans. What a stupid dream!"

He felt old and tired, but he also felt something else. It was a strange feeling—like a voice inside him. Joseph remembered what his grandfather had said about migration and the Ospreys and the Purple Martins, that every year the birds heard a special voice telling them to go home to the place where they were born.

So Joseph packed his bags, said good-bye to his friends and rode the train to North Vancouver. It was a long journey and he felt very tired. When he arrived at his boyhood home near the inlet, where his family still lived, he became sick and for a long time he lay in bed, not eating, not sleeping, just looking out of the window and remembering...

"He has come home to die," his family said.

One day while he lay in bed thinking back over his life, Joseph remembered some more of his grandfather's wise words: "Whenever you feel sad, or tired, or ill, go outside and let nature take care of you."

Joseph realized he could hardly breathe. The room was too warm—he longed to be outside, to feel the cool breeze on his face, to smell the spring blossoms, to let nature take care of him.

He got out of bed, got dressed and ate some food, then opened the door and slowly walked out into the bright May sunshine. He felt weak but strangely excited. The words spoken by the Osprey and Purple Martin in his dream came back to him: "We are going to a special place on the inlet, where the humans have made a miracle."

Joseph felt a strong desire to see what was left of the marshes and mudflats where he had spent so many happy hours with his grandfather—the place where he had first seen the Osprey and the Purple Martins all those years ago.

Everything along the beach had changed so much, it was difficult for Joseph to remember where he had walked with his grandfather so long ago. But some strange force was guiding him along, making him walk in a certain direction. To his surprise he was drawn to a big blue building just off the highway. "More concrete!" he thought. But there was something different about this place. For one thing, it was surrounded by young maple trees. That made him remember the maple woods and the time he had lost Grandfather and learned about the magic of nature. As he walked past the blue building, Joseph noticed that the landscape was becoming greener and more natural. Then he realized that he wasn't alone. A Black-tailed Deer and a family of Canada Geese were sharing the path, and wasn't that a coyote peering at him from the woods? Then Joseph saw a tall, grey-haired man working in a place filled with young trees and plants in pots.

"What is this place?" he asked the man. "What is going on here?"

"This is the last small piece of wetland left on the North Shore," said the man. "Many people worked hard to save it for the birds and wildlife, and now we are planting trees and shrubs—trying to make it the way it was many years ago."

"But I used to come here many years ago and it didn't look like this. It was all marshes and mudflats, down to the sea and all along the inlet," said Joseph.

"We have started to re-create the marshes, and if you keep walking you will come to the mudflats," said the man. "Come, I will show you."

He started walking away from the blue building, along a trail toward the beach. Eventually he stopped at an open space with a wide view of the inlet. Most of the mudflats had gone, but not here! Joseph's heart lifted with joy as he saw the mudflats—just as they had been when he was a boy.

Then the man pointed to a huge nest sitting on a sheet of wood that someone had nailed to the top of a wooden pole, and Joseph saw a sudden flash of white as a female Osprey flew overhead. *"Piu-piu-piu,"* she called. *"Pseek-pseek pseek-pseek,"* her mate called back, as he dived toward the sea after a fish.

Out of the corner of his eye Joseph saw a burst of purple-blue. *"Tchew-wew, pew-pew,"* called the Purple Martins as they headed for a wooden nest box someone had built for them.

It was as if the birds were welcoming him home and singing with joy at having homes of their own to come back to. Joseph realized that this was the special place he had dreamed about, the place where humans really had made a miracle for the birds and animals—the place called Maplewood Flats!